Cream Cake

For Flora and Michael

Cream Cake

Chris Barton
and Dee Shulman

RED FOX

If you were a cream cake,

I would eat you in one bite.

If you were a fire-breathing dragon,

we could fight.

If you were a rocket,

I would blast you into space.

If you were a galloping horse,

I'd let you win the race.

If you were a big potato,

you'd go in my sack.

If you were a smelly skunk –

hey! Give my glasses back.

If you were a present,

I'd unwrap you – one, two, three.

If you were a dolphin,

ou could splash around the sea.

If you were a crocodile,

I'd stay clear of your teeth.

If you were a bouncy dog,

I'd tickle you underneath.

If you were a precious stone,

I'd rub you till you shone.

If you were a teapot,

I would put your cosy on.

If you were a little bird,

towards your nest we'd creep.

But as you're just my baby boy, I'll ...

sshh – he's gone to sleep!

A Red Fox Book

Published by Random House Children's Books
20 Vauxhall Bridge Road, London SW1V 2SA

A division of Random House UK Ltd
London Melbourne Sydney Auckland
Johannesburg and agencies throughout the world

First published in 1992 by The Bodley Head Children's Books

Red Fox edition 1994

Text © Chris Barton 1992
Illustrations © Dee Shulman 1992

Printed in Singapore

RANDOM HOUSE UK Limited Reg. No. 954009